Hope

Morgan Barker, the lead character of Non Friction and brilliant author of Our Story, has all but recovered from the heartache caused by Emma. But when his company's accounting firm sends a beautiful young woman named Hope to inquire about some suspicious account practices, Morgan finds himself lured back into the beautiful story that he created and wanted to forget about. Except this new story is different than Morgan's unpublished, never-seen-before version. Read deeper into Olivia and Oliver's ongoing and difficult love affair, their secret moments and the struggle that kept them apart for so long.

HOPE
a novella

MORGAN PARKER

© 2014 QuoteStork Media, Inc.
ISBN 978-0-9917648-3-9

This is a work of fiction. All characters, conversations, circumstances and incidents are products of the author's imagination. Any and all references to real products, objects, locations, events, locations and people are meant to lend the reader a sense of authenticity but are used fictitiously.

With the exception of quoted text used in a published review, no part of this work can reproduced without the written permission of QuoteStork Media, Inc..

Follow Morgan Parker on Facebook.

Also by Morgan Parker:

Non Friction

Textual Encounters Series

Textual Encounters: The Christine + Jake Affair

Textual Encounters: 2

Coming Soon From Morgan Parker:

Textual Encounters III

Sick Day

Author's Note

Like a lot of events in my life, this story wasn't planned. It came about because a small group of incredibly supportive friends, readers, fans and bloggers urged me to pursue *Our Story*, which was introduced in *Non Friction*, the novel that, in most cases, brought this little group together in the first place.

Although I was heavily invested in *Sick Day* at the time, I figured a short about Olivia & Oliver's short love story could be easily written over the course of a weekend. However, it took much longer than that and the short became a novella. And I realized that although Olivia & Oliver's love story lasted a short time (in life), there was enough of a story to fill multiple novels. After all, that was the original, raw concept for *Our Story*.

Hope is dedicated to the small group that inspired it, the Morganettes. It's a tribute to everything that *Non Friction* was (the story that brought us together, the conception point for Olivia & Oliver) as well as a catalyst for everything that lies ahead (namely *Sick Day*).

Prologue

Hope

Judging a book by its cover isn't a bad thing; we do it all the time, and that's exactly what I did when I picked up a copy of *Sextual Encounters* on the recommendation of a close friend. And it was exactly what I did when I had the opportunity to meet with Morgan for a professional matter at the tech company where he worked.

Sitting across from him in his office, I wondered how someone with such a beautiful writing style could spend a workweek buried in paperwork and numbers and everything else we do as accountants, all of it for nothing but a paycheck that helped him forget the girl he loved. I had heard that he once said, "You aren't my words, you're my numbers, you're all of my numbers," or something equally gag worthy. Now he had business cards with CPA behind his name.

Based on the chaotic exhibit of spreadsheets, account statements and calculator tape strewn about his office, I wondered how he wasted his sappy words now. On this career of his? In fact, having read his amazing novel, I believed that this slightly overweight mess of a creature might not look the part, but he clearly possessed the most beautiful soul alive.

"I'm sure I have those receipts right here," he said, shuffling through one pile and then moving to the next. "This place is a fucking mess," he went on, mostly mumbling to himself. "I fucking hate paper. I swear we own a mill somewhere on this fucking planet."

Yes, Morgan swore a lot. I knew that coming in today.

At last he turned around, his face serious. "You'll have to come back," he said, shocking me because he hadn't used the f-word in that last statement.

"Listen," I said. "Your company pays my firm something like $500 per hour to make sure your accounting practices don't cross that imaginary line into the IRS's red zone, which is where your company is flirting right now. That means big fines and potential prison terms."

He laughed. "Five hundred fucking dollars per

hour?"

I shrugged. Morgan had a disarming way about him. I bet he could talk his way into any woman's- I snapped my attention back to the task at hand. "Yeah, I think so. It's a lot of money. Anyway, my point is that I can just sit around all day, but I'd like to have lunch with you in an hour, and that isn't something I can do until you provide those invoices."

"Lunch?" he asked. He leaned forward on his desk, all-business now. "You should know that I'm not one of those guys that fucks on a first date." He seemed serious about that for all of about two seconds, and then he laughed out loud.

I didn't even crack a grin. Instead, I waved at the mess on his desk. "Please, Morgan. You need to focus so I can do my job and you can get back to yours."

His Adam's apple bobbed as he gulped at the severity of my presence here then set back to work. I watched him make an even greater mess, then dig into a couple of drawers in his credenza – he hadn't thought to look there all morning, why now? – and at one point, I caught a glimpse of perspiration on his forehead. I knew the prospect of having lunch would ignite that inner spark, but I also knew that no matter how much literary talent this mega-perv had, he wasn't truly qualified to run an accounting department at a hi-tech firm. He didn't deserve this job, he didn't belong here.

"Here we go," he said, producing a thick folder and smacking it on the desk. He was proud of himself and, honestly, I was a little surprised too. I hadn't expected much from him.

I glanced down at the folder, opened it up and scrolled through some of the invoices. It looked legitimate.

Morgan stood up and pushed his arms into his suit jacket. "What do you say we get an early start on lunch?"

The gourmet sandwich restaurant had an old-school character, with a tiled floor straight out of the fifties, faux-leather booth seats that looked real, and a sandwich menu that could make any lunch snob blush. I ordered a half sandwich with a diet Coke; Morgan ordered a full sandwich that put a smile on his face just saying its name.

"So," he said as the waitress took our menus away. "How long have you been in the game, Hope?"

"Just a year," I told him.

He pushed a douchebag whistle out through his

lips. I didn't like him, but I *knew* him. "Five hundred dollars an hour and they send a fucking rookie. Nice."

His arrogance didn't intimidate me. Matt's boss intimidated me; his parents intimidated me. Guys like Morgan who wrote love stories to appeal to women readers, they were snakes. Garter snakes at that.

He nodded at my engagement ring. "Normally I'm on the receiving end of this, but that's big, Hope."

Cute. So cute I vomited in my mouth and pulled a long sip from my glass of water. "I should be frank with you, Morgan."

"Yeah, I'd like that."

"I know you."

"I get that a lot, too," he admitted.

"Oh?"

"Yeppers." Leaning closer to me like this was some big conspiracy, he waved me closer and whispered, "I have this habit of showing up in women's dreams. I've obviously been in yours."

Okay, *that* was pretty funny. I laughed and tried not to snort, but I couldn't hold it down entirely and a small pork-ish sound escaped.

"Fuck, you're super cute when you talk pig to

me," he said. Although he complimented me while simultaneously insulting me, I decided that this lunch had to change direction. Fast.

"I have a question, Morgan. I hope you don't mind…"

"I'm an open book when it comes to beautiful women," he admitted.

Yeah, uh huh. "Why did Olivia die?"

The sudden silence in the world suggested that I had either gone deaf or God had pressed the *mute* button on life. Morgan stared back at me with wide, frightened eyes, like I had just caught him stepping out of the shower.

Now it was my turn wear the Arrogance Cape. "It was a touching scene at the hospital. Chapter 29, wasn't it? But it was a love a story, and love stories don't end like that."

By now, all of the color had drained off his face. Well, almost all of the color – his cheeks were rosy and flushed. "How…? Do you…?"

I gave him a smile. "Emma Payne. We went to high school together." I leaned forward on the table, bringing that cape with me. "I know everything, Morgan."

Our sandwiches arrived and I dug in, famished

from the travelling and from having delivered this low blow to the man whose stories had put equal doses of smiles and tears on my face with *Sextual Encounters* and, of course, *Our Story*. I loved- no, I *fucking* loved *Our Story*.

"You're not eating?" I asked as I reached the halfway mark on my own sandwich.

"I think I'll, uh, take mine to go."

I shrugged and kept eating.

"How's, uh…" he cleared his throat. "How's Emma? She doing alright?"

I swallowed what was in my mouth, wiped my fingertips and lips with the napkin and then reached into my laptop bag. I pulled out a manuscript that was bound by one of those monster-sized clamps with a cardstock cover and four words on it: *Our Story: My Version*.

"Did she write this?" he asked, taking the sixty-nine pages from me. "This is from Emma, isn't it?" He flipped through a few pages, read a sentence here and there. Some paragraph or dialogue mid-way through the manuscript ignited a fire behind those eyes. "She still loves me," he admitted, his voice low and soft.

Another slow sip of water. I was in no hurry. "I'd love to know how many nights per week you sit at your computer, look at that screen and contemplate clicking that publish button. Or how, in those moments of loneliness and boredom, you look at your phone and wonder why she hasn't sent you another one of those texts."

He grabbed a fry from his plate. "I'm not even fucking hungry."

"You've got a twisted view on love, Morgan." I poked the manuscript's cover. "Read that, okay? Next time I see you, which will probably be in four to six weeks based on the turnaround times at the office, I want to know what you think."

And then I stood up, grabbed my bag and left him with a wave.

"Wait," he said, so I returned to the booth.

"I wasn't going to order dessert, if that's what you're wondering," I said.

He shook his head, no. "I *always* wonder why she hasn't texted me. I sit awake at night thinking that I should have fought for her. Fought harder." He rubbed his hands through his hair, clearly distressed. "We had a promise, Hope."

I couldn't help but let the grin surface. "A promise?"

"Yeah, a fucking promise. It's like a-"

"I know what a promise is, goob. But let me tell you something. 'Promise' is just a word, and any one word means nothing by itself. So your word? You may as well have used 'crank,' instead."

That confused him.

"Happy reading," I said, then added under my breath, "douchebag," as I left.

Chapter 1

- Olivia -

When Oliver drew the sheets away from me, I felt vulnerable. My body, completely exposed to this man, quivered at the touch of his fingertips, as he slid them across my lower abs, moving them slowly from one hip to the other. His eyes were blazing blue with hunger; they had transformed from their regular gray, to this color I considered mine. He never had blue eyes like those for anyone else. Only me.

He bit down on his lip, circling his fingers a little farther south toward my honey. Yes, I've called my vag "honey" since I first met Oliver because he always left me feeling sweet and sticky.

"I need you," I whispered just loudly enough for him to hear me.

His eyes moved from my honey to my face, and there was recognition there, like maybe he had forgotten all about the rest of me. Easing himself onto me, he pressed his lips to mine and kissed me hard. His tongue pushed its way into my mouth, forceful and starving for me. I moaned, knowing nothing else could satisfy that hunger of his like I could. Wrapping my arms around him, I raised my legs and pulled his erection against me, knowing I was wet enough to leave my mark on the outside of his boxer-briefs. With a gentle thrust against me, I moaned again, and then used my feet to strip him, set him free.

"I need you," he said, reaching down and rubbing the tip of his dick against my eager core. "Olivia, I need-"

I pressed my finger to his lips, reached down and grabbed him, nudging his own hand away. As much as I enjoyed the thought of him stroking himself to my pictures and words, I didn't want him touching himself now. Only my hands should be touching him so that his own hands could-

And then I felt his fingers between my legs again. His thumb found my clit, and he massaged me in a soft, circular motion. I panted, opening my eyes (I hadn't realized I'd closed them in the first place) and found him staring at me. He smiled, let go of my honey and then put his hand over mine, which was still stroking his rigid shaft.

"I love you, Olivia Warren. I always will."

"Then love me now," I whispered, pulling him closer then sliding myself onto him, arcing my neck and losing myself in the love of the moment, the sensation of his patient thrusts, his lips against my neck, his heavy breathing on my skin.

I lost myself to everything that was Oliver, and it was unlike anything I had ever known. I lost myself to love, and that was something I would bring with me to my deathbed.

Chapter 2

Behind the shower's steamed-up glass, Oliver sang some kind of song in a tune so awful I didn't recognize where it belonged. The lyrics did nothing to stir any familiarity at all. I chuckled as I stood at the mirror, bringing the mascara to my eyes and making sure the lashes didn't stick together. We had settled into something of a routine over the course of the weekend while I allowed myself to exist in absolute denial. Tomorrow he would return to his wife and I would return to an empty apartment and cry my face off, while I entertained the most torturous of images… images of Oliver creating memories with his family, memories that would keep him forever loyal to a woman he claimed to no longer love.

"Olivia, the smell of LeLabo soap will always remind me of you," Oliver said under the spray.

"I'm glad I've stained you."

"Only my heart," he replied.

"Hurry up, I'm ready." I reached into the shower and turned the water temperature so low that Oliver's singing rose an octave.

"I'm gonna get you," he said, laughing like the good sport that he was.

Chapter 3

Our dinner date tonight was aboard one of those monstrous ocean-ready yachts. It had been Oliver's idea to take advantage of Miami's unique dining options, thought we might as well splurge on an adventurous last evening together before returning to our respective lives. Once everyone was on board, we were ushered to our window table and served a glass of sparkling wine while the crew prepared to sail this beast into the Atlantic.

"We don't deserve this," I told Oliver as the big yacht pushed off the dock. "We should never have allowed things to get this far."

He raised his glass as if in a toast, and at first I thought he might be dismissing what I had just said. "Sometimes, love brings us into the darkest corners of our lives," he told me. "But we survive because love guides us through the fears and uncertainties. And other times, love brings us into the brightest sunshine, the most absolute happiness we will ever know."

Our eyes locked. I expected more, but when he said nothing else, I simply surrendered to the laughter gurgling up from my belly. "What are you saying? That made no sense at all!"

He placed his glass down and reached across the table to take my hands in his. "You missed the point, Olivia."

"Yes. Yes, I think I did."

He shook his head at me, but it wasn't dismissive or condescending or anything like that. I amused him in so many ways, and I loved that I had that kind of impact on him. It meant he would come back for more smiles, more happiness. More… me.

"It's love," he explained. "Whether we deserve this or not, whether this turns out to be the darkest day of our lives or the brightest happiness, we've been guided by love. How can we go wrong when we're guided by love, Olivia?"

It was difficult to argue with his rationale, much easier to just swallow it, let it sink in and sway me. After all, my body was still raw and humming from the love we had made earlier today. And just thinking about that passion, about him grunting as he released himself inside me, clutching my hands above my head and struggling to look into my eyes as he admitted his love for me….

I crossed my legs the other way, lifted his hand to my lips and kissed his knuckles, right above his wedding band.

"I'm afraid this will end in heartbreak," I confessed. "For me. My heart aches at the thought of being without you."

"I feel the same way, Olivia. It's worth it, though. A lifetime of heartache is worth the weekend we've had together. Absolutely."

"I disagree," I said, quietly taking my hands back so I could sip a little more wine and fidget with the napkin in my lap. "It hurts when you trust someone else with your heart. When you need them and they're not there for you. I think I'd rather live without that pain."

"What's the greater tragedy, Olivia? Living an entire life without ever tasting this kind of love, without even knowing it exists? Or taking a broken heart to your grave, knowing that, at the very least, you've had an opportunity to love someone wholly and completely? Hmm?"

I didn't even have to think that one through. "I'd rather never know this kind of love exists," I admitted. "You can't crave something you've never tasted, Oliver."

"Your view is wrong," he chuckled. "Because for as long I know you're alive, my heart will know it…" his words trailed off and he sat back in his seat, staring out the window toward the Miami skyline with the clouds turning purple as the sun made its final descent.

"Love hurts, plain and simple," I explained to him. "It destroys people. Our love hurts and it's going to destroy us. If I had known our love would lead us to this moment, I would have opted out of it."

"But you're here," he argued. "And because of that, I have to believe that your heart has found its home too."

"And where's that, Oliver? Where is my heart's home?"

"With mine," he said. His face was as serious as I had ever seen it. "Our hearts belong together. And without yours, mine will stop beating."

Chapter 4

Returning to Las Vegas, I allowed the afterglow to emanate from my pores. After the weekend in Miami with Oliver, I felt unstoppable. The owner of the mortgage brokerage where I worked noticed right away.

"Did you get laid, Olivia?" he asked. As a short and chubby man, I couldn't imagine him seeing much action, which was probably why he asked about mine so often now that I was officially separated.

I gave him a wink and continued to my office. With over $4 million in closings this month, I could afford this moment of quiet. While my laptop booted, I picked up the phone and dialed Oliver's work number, just to listen to his voicemail.

"Hope you're doing well, my Love. Just getting into work and I can't stop smiling." I turned around in my chair and stared out my office window at the monstrosities known as the Vegas strip. "You need to call me as soon as you get this message." I heaved a deep breath. "I love you,

Oliver."

I hammered away at my keyboard, tapping out the final details of another mortgage application that would close in a few months. Even though I was recognized as a top-performing mortgage agent, at this stage of the game the objective was to ensure I had enough closings to sustain my lifestyle now that I was single again.

The morning passed without a return call from Oliver. I contemplated canceling my lunch meeting in case he called while I was out, but because I was lunching with one of my most-generous, top-selling real-estate agents (who also happened to be one of my best friends) it didn't make sense to risk the revenue stream (or friendship). Besides, if Oliver really wanted to speak with me, he would call my cell.

We ate at a national chain with substandard grub and poor service, but the lazy service allowed us time to talk about some of the upcoming changes at the larger mortgage lenders, their relaxed down-payment standards, increased geographic concentration limits and so on. And Jannie told me about some of the local sales trends and projections. Fun stuff.

"Heard you were away," she broached at last. "And

judging by that smile you've had on your face this entire time, I'm guessing you weren't away with Tim for a reconciliation weekend."

It had been my first weekend away since Tim and I had split up.

"So who is he, Olivia? A banker? Another real estate agent?" she hissed. "You better not be cheating on me."

I chuckled, shaking my head. Jannie and I had known each other since high school. She had been the maid of honor at my wedding to Tim six years ago. Like everyone else, Jannie disliked Tim for his Neanderthalism and rough edges; she had just been quieter about it than others and was even mildly supportive of my desire for him to measure up to his potential.

Anyway, a failed marriage was never a happy story, but still... I had watched Jannie burn through two husbands, two miscarriages and two bankruptcies (not in that order) in that same six-year period. For as much heartache as she had seen, Jannie's passion for life motivated me.

"It's nothing," I told her at last. "He's married and he lives in Chicago. It's..." I sighed, not believing the reality of my own words, but wondering if maybe those words spoke the greater truth than the hopeful and optimistic messages from my heart. "It's nothing."

Jannie frowned, looking down at her placemat. "Married, huh?"

"It's complicated," I told her, and it was. Oliver had two children and there was nothing "wrong" with his wife. In fact, to me she seemed like the perfect wife. Oliver's biggest complaint was that the weekend he met me, she had taken their kids to her parents' summerhouse in Wisconsin; it had been their wedding anniversary weekend. And of course, the kids complicated matters because Oliver loved them and refused to let them grow up in a broken family.

"Let me guess," Jannie said, keeping her voice confidential-level quiet but making sure I heard her clearly. "He told you that he'll leave her when the kids are old enough. Once they're off to college. And he doesn't want to break her heart because she's been loyal to him while he has been building his career." When her eyes met mine, she knew. "Olivia, what are you doing with a married man?"

It came out in one long, run-on sentence. "The way he touches me, the way he kisses me and makes me laugh and fills me with hope, it all makes me breathe, it makes me happy, it never stops and I know this will never end, and if all I ever get is the occasional weekend between now and the time his daughter is off to college, that's perfectly fine with me, because just closing my eyes-" and at this part, I closed my eyes, "-I see him and I feel him and I know he's here with me, some part of him, and the world is perfect again and I'm fine, I'm really fine, and-" I opened my eyes and chuckled at the bored sneer on Jannie's face, "-and, and I have never known love, Jannie, never like this and never again, he is everything I'll ever need, now and in the future." I drew in a large gulp of hair. "Jannie, I hope you find this kind of love someday."

She put her finger into her mouth, as if trying to force herself to vomit.

"You don't think this can work?" I asked.

"I'm sorry." She averted her eyes again, so I reached across the table and gave her hand a kind squeeze.

"Why?"

"Olivia, these things never turn out well. For anyone. He'll keep stringing you along. Think about this. You'll spend your life waiting for a phone call that will never come. And when it comes, he'll just want to fuck. And when those calls stop, you'll be stuck curled up in a corner, crying and rocking and holding your knees to your chest."

I laughed at the visual, but when she refused to join in, I stopped.

"Olivia, he's had you. And he's a jerk for it. I'm sorry for saying that, but he is. Do you want to be with a man who cheated on his wife, who risked his marriage and his relationship with his two children? Nobody wants that. You don't deserve to be second in any man's life. You should be first. And right now, even though he cheated on his poor wife, you're still second because he went home to *her*."

We engaged in a mild staring contest next. I hated to admit it, but Jannie had made a good point.

"Remember Raj?" she asked, sitting back in our booth and allowing a dirty smirk to cross her tight lips. "I loved that man and every pulsating orgasm he gave me. He loved me like a porn star, he could make me see stars by using his tongue alone. Damn, I'm getting wet just talking about him."

We both giggled, but for different reasons. If only Jannie knew how Oliver made me feel; not just my body, but my spirit. He owned me, and that feeling comforted me.

"My point with Raj is simply that it doesn't matter how much you love him, or any married man. All that matters is how much he loves you. And if he stays with his wife, the message is that he loves her more." She shook her head with a calm sadness. "I loved Raj more than both of my ex husbands combined, and it sure made me feel good at the time. But going home to an empty house, not knowing when he would find time to get away from the wife he didn't love like he claimed to love me? Not knowing when he would text or call next…? There's no loneliness like that, Olivia."

Which reminded me to check my phone, make sure the alerts weren't set to silent because Oliver should have responded to my voicemail message by now. I saw that, despite a couple of emails from clients and lenders, I hadn't missed anything.

"He hasn't written or called, has he?"

No, he hadn't. But I smiled back at her because I knew that call would arrive this afternoon, probably at the worst possible moment.

"Olivia, you need to put this where it belongs." She leaned forward on the table. "And that's in your past."

Chapter 5

Two days later, I rolled over in bed and picked up the phone. I called in sick and then turned the ringer off and closed my eyes. I hadn't slept in two days and I doubted that I would sleep at all today. Heartbreak was an amazing amphetamine, except it left you spent.

Oliver refused to answer my calls, ignored my messages and left me here like all of the other whores that worked in Vegas. I hated him. I fucking hated everything about him.

But that morning, while I lay curled up on my bed, I finally let go of that hatred. I allowed the memory of his smiling face to cut through my visions of ruining his life – strangling him, slapping him, watching him plea with me to keep our affair secret from his wife, and about half a million or so other fantasies exactly like those – and I found peace.

"Why did you do this to me, Oliver?" I wept as I tugged the corner of my bed comforter over my shoulder and wrapped it around my chest. It felt like his arms around me and, as much as I wished the world's worst pain upon him, the made-up memory of Oliver holding me in his arms helped me find the sleep and peace I had been seeking since Monday.

Chapter 6

Oliver

It wasn't my fault. We had a promise, a plan. Wasn't my fault Olivia got a little trigger happy and bailed on her marriage more than a decade ahead of schedule. And now, while I sat on the train heading into Chicago, I wondered whether I would find her on my voicemail this morning. Two weeks ago, Olivia had left increasingly more panicked messages for me, but then they ended last Monday. Would today bring her voice back? Or was she gone for good?

"Hey, Oliver," the Metra Conductor said, taking my ticket. "Nothing feels better than a Thursday."

"That's because you don't work on Fridays, Vlad," I mumbled back.

He chuckled, patting my shoulder and moving on.

"Enjoy your weekend."

I hadn't slept in days and the shadows under my swollen eyes confirmed that. Grabbing my Blackberry, I accessed the jAppe messaging service. I refused to scroll through the photos folder because seeing her face would crush me. Her last message had been laced with enough anger that reading it left her fingerprints around my throat – yeah, she was *pissed*. Crazy was more like it.

I typed a quick response to Olivia.

> Me: Olivia, what has gotten into you? I thought when we said goodbye in Miami, we agreed on a break because you know what these Olivia-binges do to me, and you said they do the same to you? And now you're going on like a lunatic. Fuck, I'm sorry I can't leave my wife yet. She doesn't deserve this and it's bad enough I cheated on her – not sexually (which is bad, yes) but emotionally. I love a woman who lives 1,500 miles away and I can't be with her. It's not fair to my wife, or my kids, or me that you own 100% of me, my thoughts and love.

> I considered saying fuck it, I'm done. Because leaving you was one thing, but coming home was like stepping into a coffin; I couldn't breathe, I couldn't exist because that was my

entire life with*out* you. I'm fucked now, you see?

But last night at dinner, after my wife and son cleared the table, my princess put her little hand on my knee and looked me straight in the eyes and asked me why my heart was crying. Even at eight, my little daughter sees that I'm hurting here... why can't you see that? Why can't you help to make these days less agonizing?

You're killing me, Olivia. Stop with the crazy. I'm coming to Vegas at the end of the month – you know this already – and we can talk then.

I deliberated sending the message for all of two minutes, but like the hundreds of others I had written over the past two days, I refused to fall into her waiting hands. I questioned her doubts, her craziness... and then I questioned my own.

I tucked the phone back into my pocket. I needed to get my head into the game, I needed to focus on work and bluffing my way through my marriage for the next two weeks before I travelled to Vegas for the second time since meeting my soul mate.

Chapter 7

I left the meeting room, knowing too well that my face had turned the color of powder-white snow.

"Oliver," my boss called out. I kept going, smashing into the reception area and then out of our office into the hallway to the elevators. I pounded on the call button, then gave up and slammed into the stairwell. I hurried down the stairs two at a time. And when it struck me that I had forty-something more stories to go before reaching street level, I stopped. The silence ate at me like acid and, with my back against the wall of the 43rd floor landing, I lowered myself to the ground.

The emotion rocked through my body. I raised my hands to my face and let it all pour out, my poorly suppressed sobs enhanced by the echoes bouncing off of the stairs. If anyone had entered the stairwell, whether on this floor or in the lobby, they would have turned around and walked away. When it came to crying, I wasn't graceful. At all.

That meeting had been about my employment with

the firm. Well, not just mine, but everyone in the risk management group. We were done. I would be one of the last to go, but the decision had been made to terminate the entire unit as it wasn't considered a "core" business of the firm's.

"Fuck, Olivia," I whispered, wiping my eyes like a child who hadn't received the birthday gift he had asked for. But instead of not getting the gift, the reality was that I *had* been given the gift. Up until two minutes ago, I *had* been booked for the Vegas conference and I would have seen that gift. I had hoped to sneak up on Olivia, pin her against a wall, a tree, a car, even a bed, and make sure she knew beyond any other truth in this life, that our love could and would withstand any test, any amount of time. Our love was stronger than any metal, any stone, and it would last longer than time itself. Why didn't she see this, why didn't she believe it?

At that moment, my Blackberry buzzed with the two short vibrations of an incoming text. I knew what to expect before looking at the message, before opening jAppe. And just knowing that she had texted me brought a smile to my face. Because that was how our love worked – distance and time meant nothing. We co-existed and we were one, even after that crazy dry spell.

    I opened jAppe and read her message. I was already teary eyed, how much worse could it get?

> Olivia: I miss you. I'm hurt. I'm angry. I love you and I hate you. I know why you ignored my messages, and it's why I stopped sending them last week. I don't know why you haven't responded. But this week has been good. Really good, because I'm sleeping. As good as it could get, really. But today? Something's different and I can feel it. Like you've slipped away.
>
> When you were in Vegas last time, I left Tim. Earlier than agreed, yes. And I don't expect you to leave your wife. No, I don't. Instead, I expect you to make more memories with your family. Memories you won't ever want to let go of, and I'm fine with that. But don't think a day passes when I don't cry for you, Oliver. Because every day IS you. I miss my days.

    Sometimes, it isn't the words so much as the message. And in this case, the message that Olivia had written to me told me everything I needed to know: Like me, she couldn't control or ignore this connection of ours. And like me, she was a little fucked up, too.

As if my life needed yet another fucked up plot twist, the Blackberry buzzed again – *bzzt-bzzt*.

This time, I didn't smile.

Olivia: I'm determined to get my days back, Oliver. I didn't mean to worry you with my last message or with any of the others from last week. I'm happy, you should know that. I know it's early, but I've finally agreed to have dinner with Carlo Antonio, the guy I mentioned to you in Miami. He sold a software company to Google a few years ago and is now doing programming at one of the casinos. You can look him up, he's well known in the industry and he's single so you have no more risk of me going crazy on broken promises and coming to fuck up your happy life. Take care of yourself, Oliver.

If I had said that I had been expecting *that* message, I would have been lying.

Chapter 8

I hadn't told my wife about losing my job. So every morning, I kept getting dressed in a business suit, ironing my shirts, then hurrying to the train station (or asking for a ride if it happened to be raining) and pretending to get on the Metra into Chicago. And every night, I would return to the house at the same time, just in case she beat me home. I would kiss her on the forehead when I entered through the front doors and found her preparing dinner, and then tell her about my shitty day, making it up arbitrarily. But today was a little different. After kissing her, I lingered in the kitchen and watched her from behind as she rinsed vegetables at the sink.

"Everything okay, Oliver?" Like she had eyes in the back of her head.

"I've got to make a trip to Toronto next week." I sighed. "Horrible timing. The worst."

She turned from the vegetables and studied me, placing her hands on her hips. Had she figured out my charade? Had she called the office instead of my cell phone today and discovered that the Risk unit had been relocated to Head Office?

I shrugged and started to walk away, grabbing a slice of the uncooked garlic bread she had been working on.

"You know I hate Canada," I said with my mouth half full. "It's bloody cold there," which was a lie because the Chicago weather was a million times worse than the worst I had ever endured in Toronto.

"What's happening in Toronto?" she asked.

With my back to her, I finished chewing what I had in my mouth. The truth was that the Toronto Sheraton was hosting an author event that I learned about while creeping on Olivia Warren's Facebook page. She would be among the attendees. I needed to see her again, needed to see those eyes and find out if this Antonio bullshit was for real.

"I mean, you mentioned that the big Vegas trip was cancelled last month for budgetary reasons. But now Toronto comes up out of the blue. Seems odd; the Vegas convention is bigger, isn't it?"

I nodded my agreement. Yes, the trip to Toronto would cost almost twice as much as the trip to Vegas. But I hadn't been prepared to visit Olivia last month after losing my job, my mind. When she texted me about that Antonio douchebag, I figured it was best to stay away. My self-pity could keep me company just fine.

"Must be an important, big conference, huh?" she persisted.

At last, I turned around and faced her. "It's not a conference. It's a small meeting with one of our clients. It's a two-night visit and when I get back, I'm told the travel will be limited. Very limited." I shrugged. "I'm going upstairs to go get changed. Did you pick up the dry-cleaning?"

She didn't answer me, but I didn't care.

As I climbed the stairs, I checked the Blackberry to see if a message had snuck through without me noticing the vibrations. No, nothing. It hurt to think about Olivia in Vegas, not even concerned about me or wondering how my days without her have been.

But it hurt more to think that she had replaced me so quickly and easily.

Chapter 9

I hadn't slept well last night.

The bumpy one-hour flight from Chicago to Toronto had reminded me of when Olivia and I met. Neither of us liked to fly, and the turbulence meant we had both had a bit to drink. Why the airline had buddied us up together remained a mystery, but at some point during that first weekend together we hypothesized that old-fashioned Fate had been involved somewhere along the line. If we hadn't been neighbors on that flight from Vegas to Chicago, we might have never met, and the prospect of that had never really sunk in until now, as I rode a cab from the Toronto airport to the Sheraton Hotel.

After paying the driver, I stepped into the busy and vast Sheraton lobby. I felt it immediately – my heart rate quickened, I became incredibly warm (it truly felt like a fucking sauna in there) and I could… I don't know, I could *sense* Olivia's presence. At first, I glanced everywhere, the world seeming to spin around me as I searched the busy lobby for her face, for a sign of her. Somewhere. I wanted to shout her name, get everyone to shut up and point her out to me.

"Hey, watch it," a younger brunette in heels and tight jeans said as she pushed past me, heading toward the escalators with a group of five other women. They wore lanyards with the Toronto Author Event's logo on them.

I watched the younger women for a beat, taking deep, calculated breaths.

Olivia.

I closed my eyes and concentrated hard. I could hear and feel people walking around me to get to their destination – the bar to the right side, the elevators a little farther into the lobby, the reception desk to the left, or anywhere else – but their presence didn't phase me. At all.

I simply listened to my heart – *thump-thump, thump-thump* – and turned slightly to the right, toward the bar. Except when I opened my eyes, I didn't find her inside the bar (half of the tables weren't visible from here anyway). Instead, she sat in a foursome of square-edged chairs with three other women. One of them wrote madly in a notebook; another tapped away on her phone; the third one smiled and asked questions.

And then there was Olivia. She sat in a relaxed

position, her legs crossed and her long hands hanging over the edge of the chair's armrests. She flashed her smile (the other women chuckled) and composed herself for the next question – they were interviewing her. Her eyes glittered and, when she spoke next, the right side of her mouth tightened as she wrestled to maintain her composure. I caught myself staring at her, admiring her without alerting her to my presence. I wondered if this happiness was something that Antonio enjoyed every single day her spent with her.

As if on cue, the other women burst into laughter, and Olivia followed soon after. I knew how much she loved talking about her books, her stories. While stalking her Facebook earlier, I noticed that her second novel's release had been delayed. Twice. Evidently, she was on schedule to meet this third release deadline.

When a lull in the conversation settled in, Olivia allowed her attention to stray. She saw me, and our eyes locked.

Before she could recognize me and do anything about it, I reached down for my luggage and veered toward the check-in desk on the left side of the lobby. Although I had broken our little staring contest, I felt her eyes on me, digging into my back like her fingernails had the last time we were together. In Miami.

I missed Miami.

I missed Olivia.

I checked into the hotel without a problem (not that I expected one) and followed the front desk clerk's directions to my room. Once inside, I placed my carry-on on the desk, grabbed a fresh change of clothes and indulged in a hot shower. As the water washed over me, I remembered the last time I had showered away from home. Pressing my hand against the tiled wall, I realized just how wrong it looked.

Olivia's fingers belonged with mine. That last time I had found myself in under a hot hotel-room spray, her ass had been pressed up against my crotch, one hand pinning hers to the shower walls, the other pulling back on her hair.

"Fuck." I gulped a mouthful of steam, pulling my hand away from the tile and killing the water (not to mention my fantasy of fucking Olivia). I dried myself off, got changed, and returned to the lobby. It was quieter than earlier. The only people who walked through the vast lobby were couples in formal suits and gowns, and of course the women from the Toronto Author's Event looking to have a nice night out in Toronto.

I waited near the doors, watching the other authors step outside to waiting limos and cabs. As the pedestrian traffic died down, I wondered whether Olivia would even show up. And sitting there in the lobby, it finally hit me. I chuckled to myself at just how stupid I had been to not realize this sooner.

She was probably spending the evening with Antonio. Probably dinner in that revolving restaurant at the CN Tower, the same gimmicky dining experience she had enjoyed at the John Hancock that time we were together in Chicago.

The realization stung. Of course she would be spending time with her new boyfriend; the guy probably had nothing else to do but follow her around like a lost puppy dog.

"Oliver?" I heard behind me.

Her voice stilled me.

When she walked around to face me, I had to remind myself to just keep breathing. So I breathed in her white pants, breathed in her black top that revealed the black bra straps that clung to the freckled shoulder that I also breathed in. And when she smiled at me, I breathed in her bright red lips, those perfectly white teeth, and the way her eyes seemed to curl with that smile.

I was lost. Speechless.

"I thought I saw you earlier," I lied. Pushing myself to my feet, I held out my hand, but instead of taking it, Olivia allowed herself to melt into my chest.

"Hold me, Oliver," she hushed into my ear. "I've missed you more than air."

I wrapped my arms around her. I held her. And if inhaling the full essence of her wasn't enough, when she placed her head against my shoulder, I knew exactly why we were here. This was home, right here in my arms, and I knew just how foolish I had been to think either of us could ever walk away from this, from where we both belonged. And that was right here.

Together.

Now.

Chapter 10

Waking up with Olivia's hair in my face, the chaos of the past few months and change dissipated into nothingness. All that mattered was this moment, laying in this bed with the crisp white sheets over our naked bodies. As the fog dissipated from my mind, I brushed the hair out of her face and watched her come awake. The first thing she did was smile. The next, she opened her eyes and that smile brightened.

"I'm sorry," she whispered, despite that smile still plastered to her lips. "I really like Carlo."

I wiggled away from her because our night together suggested that Carlo was nothing more than a free dinner. "What about us?"

She sat up, wrapping herself with the white sheets. "Oliver, you're married. There's something like a decade between now and when I can finally have you all to myself. You don't expect me to be single that whole time, do you?"

It hurt to breathe, like I had a few broken ribs and each breath stabbed like a knife puncturing my lungs.

"Carlo's good to me, he treats me really well."

"Do you… do you love him?"

"Oliver…"

I walked away from the bed, glanced back, and then stared out the hotel room's window at the street some thirty stories below. A street car rolled past, a taxi cut someone else off. I noticed the pedestrians… seemed strange to see this many people out so early on a Saturday morning.

"You're married," she repeated from the bed.

"But I love you," I answered to the window. "I fucking love you and this is killing me."

"I'm not going to say things would be different if you weren't married, if you lived closer to me…"

I swung around. "Why not? Why won't you say that?"

"Because it's not fair to you."

I returned to the bed and sat on the corner, my naked body exposed and vulnerable to this woman who seemed to have just used me for a night of sex. Although I could count on one hand how many times we had been together, it felt like we had lived our entire lives together. Like this. In a love that felt tangible to me, yet obviously meant nothing to her.

"You said it yourself," she continued. "Your wife's not the devil. It's not fair to her either."

I stared down at my limp dick and remembered how she taken all of me in her mouth last night. I shook my head, as much at the memory as at the words she had spoken.

Olivia crawled across the mattress and brushed her hand through my hair. She may as well have been running those fingers through my soul; her touch calmed me like nothing else I had ever known.

"Remember when you sent me that text? The one where you told me about this Carlo Antonio guy?" I heaved a deep breath. I felt safe with Olivia right here with me, no matter what she had just confessed about really liking this other man, no matter how married I was, no matter how, after this weekend, I realized I might never see her again. I felt safe… period. "That day you sent the text, I found out that I would be out of a job. And two weeks later, I was walked out of my office with a box that barely defined the last eight years of my career."

"You never told me."

"I couldn't."

"You never wrote to me, Oliver." She pulled back. Her face had tightened into a pained frown. "You just ignored me, every text I sent, every message I left. What was I supposed to think? That you *love* me?"

I raised my attention to her again. "I'm here. I came for you. That's the only reason I'm here and if I had to spend the weekend hiding in my room, waiting for that one opportunity to take you aside and tell you what and how I feel… I would have been fine with that. I just needed to see you."

The hurt in her perfect face stung me.

"Do you love this guy?"

"Do you love your wife?" she spat back at me.

"I love *you*."

She studied me, softening with every second. "And I love you, Oliver." She blinked and reached out, taking me into her arms.

I held her tighter, and when I heard a soft sniffle, I knew she was crying in my arms. It broke my heart.

"Why do we doubt this?" she asked so quietly that I questioned the existence of the words. "How come I'm worried about you leaving? How come I'm supposed to trust you? How come you don't trust me?"

I grinned – she didn't love him.

"You've ruined me, I'm forever scarred by you, Oliver."

"You've made it worse for me." My words barely escaped my mouth, my throat had tightened and I felt like I was hanging on to normalcy by a very thin thread. "And this new guy…"

When she pulled back, I saw past the tears in her eyes and realized just how genuine her words had been. Trust. Love.

I nodded, understanding the message without having to hear the words. I snapped out of it.

"You have a writer's conference to get to," I said, pushing her away with a playful thrust.

She laughed and kicked at me. Nobody got hurt, but I grabbed her ankle and held it next for a heartbeat. The mood changed, the tension thickened, and I wondered if she wanted to make love. I kissed the bridge of her foot and started to work my way up her leg. But before I reached her knee, she rolled away, shaking her head at me like this was bad news, like last night hadn't happened.

"If we do this, I'll never leave your room," she said, fumbling to assemble her clothes from the floor.

I watched her get dressed and once she finished, she leaned in for a kind kiss.

"I'm finished at six," she said, fleeing from my room with a final goodbye: "I'm done at six, Oliver. Then we're going out for dinner."

I felt like such a pussy; once the door bolted shut, I grinned stupid-big and buried my face into the pillow she had used last night, inhaling her scent and wishing I could be holding the real thing.

Chapter 11

I spent the afternoon shopping for flowers and Olivia's favorite treats (she loved lemon cookies and I knew from previous visits to Toronto that the lemon-crème cookies in Canada tasted absolutely orgasmic). I also picked up a bottle of wine that had been produced at a nearby vineyard, a new pair of jeans and I even discovered a trendy little restaurant in an area called the "Distillery District," a place that accepted a bit of a bribe ($150) to assemble a private table in their kitchen area. I had planned the entire evening, arranging every little detail. The excitement radiated in long bursts of energy. Six o'clock felt like a lifetime away.

But upon returning to the hotel, I felt something was wrong. Different. Just walking into the vast lobby, I *felt* it. I chuckled at myself for trusting this love, for believing this morning's ecstasy could extend into this evening.

Despite the message my heart was sending, I returned to my room with the flowers and treats, suddenly tired and ready for a nap. A long nap from which I never wanted to awaken. And that was exactly what I did (napped), except I did awaken and it was sometime around four o'clock. In the morning.

Knowing I would not be able to find my way back to sleep, I rolled out of bed. I stumbled through the darkness to the bathroom, my entire body aching to the point where I felt ten years older. Ten *hard* years.

Staring at my reflection in the mirror, I chuckled because in ten years I hoped to be holding Olivia in my arms. How had I done this, how had I so easily lost a woman that had given herself entirely to me.

"Haven't even spoken to her!" I said to my reflection, then brought myself a little closer because I noticed the lines at my eyes, the age spreading across my jaw. I was getting old, and age was not my ally.

As if Fate sensed the pain and aching in my heart, I heard a feeble knock at the door. I knew I would find Olivia on the other side of that knock, but something felt different. In all honesty, I expected to find her drunk after having spent a night out with her author friends.

But when I yanked the door open, I found the most sobering version of Olivia I had ever seen. She wore flannel pants and a tight white tank top. She looked beautiful in a sad kind of way, with her head bowed like she did not want to look at me.

"What happened tonight?" I asked, keeping my voice low. I reached out for her, but she withdrew her hands so I couldn't touch them. "Fuck, Olivia. I had this amazing night planned out, something so beautiful... fuck. I'm dying here. I came all this way. All we had was this weekend together, and now it's coming to an end."

She acknowledged my words with a faint nod, and then stepped past me, deeper into my dark hotel room. I peeked into the hotel hallway like they do in the movies (I didn't know why) and then closed the door, locking it before joining Olivia in the darkness. She tapped the empty part of the mattress, so I sat next to her.

Deep down, I knew this meant we would not be making love tonight. It saddened me, but just spending this time with her meant more to me than any amount of sex. I had tasted her the night before, after surviving months without her. Naively, I believed I could last *years* without tasting her, so long as I knew that at the end of that stint, she would be waiting for me.

Olivia's hand skittered across the bed sheets and found my mine. She squeezed it.

And then she whispered, but before the words

could register I felt an immediate panic. "I'm sorry, Oliver. I can't wait for you."

The meaning sunk in with the calm determination of irrevocable madness. All I kept thinking about was what little time we had left. Not just this weekend in Toronto, but in our lives, and that wrecked me. I had seen my face in the mirror not even two minutes ago, I had heard the words that my heart told me. But she wouldn't be there?

I would never find another Olivia.

"It was a mistake to love you like I did last night."

I heard the tears in her voice, but a quick glance at her dry face suggested she had rehearsed her lines, probably spent the entire night alone in her room delivering them to her own reflection in a mirror that had been kinder to her than mine had been to me.

Now it was my heart's turn to break at hearing those words for the first time.

"Olivia," I said, my voice a hair louder than a whisper. "He doesn't love you like I do."

"He's also not married like you are." Rehearsed. Of course she had known I would say that – we shared a soul, or that was what Olivia had led me to believe.

"He's not permanent, he's-"

"A time filler?" she asked, and I detected a hint of hope in her question. Sometimes, hope was all you needed, so I exploited that.

"You said it. And he is. You know that's all he is."

"What if I fall in love with him?" she asked, as much for herself as for me.

"You won't. Ten years isn't a long time, Olivia."

She pulled her hand back and shook her head, almost defiantly. "It's a *very* long time. And if you can't leave your wife now, what am I supposed to think you will do once you have another photo album full of family pictures to keep you anchored in your so-called misery?"

Definitely rehearsed, *well* rehearsed. "Olivia," I begged. "You'll never find love like this."

"How do I know if I don't go looking for someone who can love me?" she let out a long sigh and stepped off the bed. "You don't expect me to wait for a promise, do you? I'm young now. I have lots to give. And I want to be loved. Weren't you the one who told me that if we don't take those risks, we'll never know? In Miami, remember?"

"Don't leave me."

"I'm sorry, Oliver. I have to. My love for you, it's not diminished. You'll know I'm thinking of you."

"I already do."

"And I'm happy for you, no matter how things turn out. I want you to be happy." She moved closer to me, took my face in her hands and forced me to look at her. "I want happiness for you. If things work out with you and your wife, and you find that love that first brought you together, I will be the happiest woman alive." A tear rolled down her cheek and those big beautiful eyes looked as glassy as marbles. "You'll know this. Because once you're happy, I'll be happy. And you'll know because... because when you and your wife are walking away from your daughter's college dorm, holding hands and smiling about having your home and lives back to yourselves, you'll feel a breeze brush across your face. It'll taste like Spring, though, not Fall, and you'll know that I sent it." Her eyes jumped across my face, and then she smiled. "Don't cry, Oliver. Please, stop crying. This might not be a happy time now, but you'll look back on tonight- this *morning* as the happiest gift I have ever given you."

She leaned forward and kissed the top of my head.

"Please don't cry," she begged.

And then she bolted from the room as if my sadness were somehow contagious.

Chapter 12

Olivia + Oliver

Forever

Arriving in Chicago, Oliver struggled with his share of heartache. Each bump on the aircraft threatened to break him into tears. So he wore sunglasses, even as he collected his baggage from the claim area and walked through the airport to the parking garage. It wasn't exactly a sunny day.

The drive home from the airport in his number-cruncher-appropriate Honda Accord with the wipers set on automatic was fucking slow. Ten minutes into the drive, traffic reduced to a congested crawl, but the drive remained uneventful. No accidents or speed traps, just a bunch of people heading into the city on a Sunday afternoon. Despite the loneliness of the ride, Oliver's memory of his weekend with Olivia kept him company.

Two hours later, he steered onto his street and rolled to a stop in his driveway, right next to his wife's SUV. Which meant she was home. Removing his sunglasses, he stared at the front door from behind the wheel. He didn't want to be home, he wanted to be with Olivia. He wondered how easily he could start the engine and just drive away. Run to Vegas. Offer himself to Olivia.

"Crazy," he muttered to himself before finally shoving the car door open, grabbing his luggage from the back seat and heading inside.

His daughter rushed to him first, and then his son. They embraced them, the noise from the television pouring into the hall and washing over him, flushing the graphic memories out of his head. He closed his eyes and sucked in a deep breath for strength. It worked. And when he opened his eyes, he found his wife watching this little scene in the front foyer.

She was unimpressed. Utterly.

When her attention rose to his face, she forced a grin.

"Welcome home, Oliver," she allowed, then unfolded her arms and headed back into the kitchen.

Once she was out of his sight, he smelled the day-long baking — brownies, date squares, even home-made bread. Tasty.

Oliver leaned down when his daughter asked him if

he had brought anything home for them. It killed him to say that he hadn't. "Toronto's not very exciting."

"The CN Tower is there," his son pointed out.

"Yes, and that's about it." He shook his head because Toronto was now synonymous with Olivia. "Sorry, kiddos. Next time." Straightening himself up, he grabbed his suitcase. "Who's gonna help me unpack my bag?"

The kids screamed and followed him upstairs to the bedroom he had been sharing with his wife for the past sixteen years.

Chapter 13

Without the benefit of having a job, Oliver was stuck spending a lot of time at home. A lot. While he still got dressed in his suits and ties for his days at an office that had dumped him, and he still took a walk downtown so that his wife thought he was heading into that office, Oliver knew he didn't have much time left to figure this out. The severance was running out and his contacts in the industry complained of a hiring freeze that threatened their friendships.

Instead of veering toward the train station, Oliver made a right turn and found his way to Barney's, a small boutique espresso chain. As he entered, he heard the clanging bell of the approaching train at the same time as the bell above the door. The barista behind the counter noticed him and leaned forward on the counter, almost seductively.

"Oliver, you're going to miss your train again."

Her name was Heather, and Heather had a fuck-me smile that lifted Oliver's grim mood. "That's alright. I'm done with the whole nine-to-five thing." I nodded at the menu board.

"The usual?"

"Make it a double shot," he answered. "I'm going to need it for the conversation I'll be having with my wife."

After Heather made change for a ten, she moved to the far end of the counter where she worked the espresso machine like a pilot manning the controls of a 747.

"So why aren't you working? By your choice or theirs, Oliver?" Heather probed as she worked the levers and steamed the skimmed milk.

"Theirs."

She finished with the machine. "Shit, that sucks. I'm sorry to hear it."

He gave her a grin to prove just how brave he was. "Things happen for a reason. I think it's a blessing. Really." He bit down on his lower lip to keep the words from spilling out.

As Heather poured the frothy milk into the cup, she glanced up and frowned. "Say it, Oliver. You've known me for over a year, I thought we told each other everything?" She chuckled.

"Soul mates, right?" He contributed to the

chuckling.

"Something like that," Heather said, as she filled the cup. While she worked with the cappuccino, Oliver noticed the tattoo on her wrist. It said: *Let Go*. He hadn't noticed Heather's simple tattoo before (he *had* been seeing her here off and on for over a year), so he chalked it up to a sign that he was seeing it now after his recent weekend with Olivia.

In fact, he felt that Olivia had managed to communicate that message to him. Somehow, some way, these words on Heather's wrist had reached him through Olivia's sheer will. *Let Go*. It hurt to see those words, so he ripped his eyes away and focused on Heather as she made an artistic heart shape with the froth.

"I could almost read too much into this," he said.

Heather pushed the cup across the counter to him. "You know something, Oliver? I'm glad you're unemployed. It's nice seeing a little more of your face."

He considered her words, pouring a bit of sugar into the cappuccino and stirring it a little longer than he needed to. He loved this place, and when he finished with the stirring, he gave Heather a thankful nod and retreated to his regular table in the back corner. In the unlikely event that his wife happened to stop in (she was more of a Starbucks junkie), she wouldn't see him there. It was a safe corner.

And safety felt good right about now.

Chapter 14

Later that week, when Oliver confessed to his wife that he had lost his job, he left out the part where he had tucked away a good chunk of his severance package in a secret bank account that she would never know about. He also left out the part where he had been unemployed for nearly a month now, as well as the part where he had travelled to Toronto to see the woman who was slowly robbing his heart and mind.

"You've been acting different, Oliver. I knew something was up."

Of course something was up – without the benefit of work-related travel, he would have to pay for his own airline tickets if he wanted to defy Hope's wishes to "Let Go" and fight for her love.

His wife shook her head, the edge of her lips curling into a smile as she stepped closer to him and stared straight into his eyes. "You should have told me this was going on at work, Oliver. I thought…" She shook her head a little more and he could read the thought that she refused to share with him.

"It's okay," he said, kissing her on the top of her head, just like Olivia had kissed him last weekend in Toronto. Now he knew what that kiss meant.

"I thought you were having an affair." She rolled her eyes, more at herself than at him. "I've been driving myself crazy."

He kissed her again and walked away, heading out to the front porch. He stood outside and stared at the dark and quiet street, the Honda in the driveway, his wife's SUV, the baseball on the front lawn that seemed illuminated by the moon. When he stared up at the sky, he watched the blinking lights of a passing airplane. Once the light was gone, he searched for another. All he saw were the stars, floating alone in the sky. He hoped for a shooting star, some kind of sign like the one he had entertained at Barney's earlier.

But there were no shooting stars for him.

The door opened and his wife joined him on the porch, wrapping her arms around him. "I'm sorry you lost your job, Oliver. I know how much it meant to you. But we'll get through this. We're titanium, aren't we?"

He heaved a long sigh, keeping his hands to

himself. Because while his wife held him and assured him with her unwavering support, all he could think about was how badly he wished it was Olivia holding him. And when he refused to blame his soft marriage on the matter of "another woman," he realized that Olivia really had little to do with his matrimonial issues. Their problems were theirs alone.

"I'll make some calls on Monday," his wife promised. "Let's enjoy the weekend with the kids. You'll have interviews before the end of next week." She kissed his shoulder and returned to the house, leaving him in the dark to wonder why he didn't have the balls to tell his wife he didn't love her anymore.

Chapter 15

For two years, Oliver woke up wondering if Olivia had forgotten about him. Yet each night, he fell asleep staring into the image of her pretty face, an image he had memorized so intensely that whenever he so much as blinked, her smile flickered across that momentary blackness. Each minute of the past two years, he had thought about her; each breath reached deep into his soul, and each moment that allowed him a taste of life, he was reminded that he existed solely for one other person: Olivia Warren.

On his lone business trip (to Vegas) since finding a new job at a big-four firm, he rented a Jeep and drove out to her address. Well, it was Antonio's address – a big ranch-style bungalow with a big front porch and cactus plants on the front lawn – but he knew Olivia had moved in with him. Killing the engine, he reclined the driver's seat and just watched the house from across the street, waiting for a glimpse of her on the other side of that wrought-iron fence.

Once the sun started to disappear behind the

mountains, the temperature started to drop as well. And that was when Olivia stepped outside with a cup of coffee. No, it was probably a latté. She settled into one of the two big old rocking chairs, and Oliver sat straighter in the driver's seat so he could catch a better glimpse of her.

Even from this distance, she embodied the purest meaning of the word "perfection." To his eyes, nothing was so beautiful as this woman and Oliver immediately hungered for her. His heartbeat accelerated and he breathed more heavily through his mouth, hoping to draw her scent onto his lips or tongue. He watched her place the latté on the porch and reach for her iPhone. She seemed to be texting someone, when Oliver had an idea of his own.

Reaching into his pocket, he found his own iPhone and, having memorized her number, he sent her a quick text: "Do you remember?"

Within moments, she received his message. Oliver knew this from Olivia's behavior. He watched her shoulders go limp and her arms collapse into her lap. The iPhone dropped onto the porch.

Frowning, he guided his attention back up to her pretty face and saw that she wept quietly in the chair. Fighting the urge to get out of the rented Jeep to console her, Oliver wondered if he had made a mistake by sending that message. He hated to see her crying, but he was grateful for the opportunity to see her, even though it looked like this.

Once Olivia regained her composure, she lifted her attention and stared straight at him. Their eyes locked and, as embarrassed as he felt about Olivia discovering him here like a Peeping Tom, he savored their connection. It felt like their staring contest lasted a long, long time, and Oliver never wanted to let it go.

But he needed to. This wasn't healthy, this wasn't right.

He had *let go*. Just like she wanted.

This was a mistake.

Once Olivia finally broke their connection so she could reach down for her latté, Oliver started the engine and drove away. But not without first glancing into the rearview mirror and finding that she had launched into a full-throttle sprint after him, stopping at the front gate that kept her douchebag's property safe from stalkers, and staring after him through the iron spindles.

He felt like he had just robbed a bank; he needed to escape. Reaching the stop sign at the end of Olivia's street, he barely braked. The tires screamed as he made his fast turn and drove toward the radiating lights that identified the Vegas strip.

Chapter 16

As Olivia walked through O'Hare, it struck her as a little juvenile that she had travelled all this way from Las Vegas. Because once Oliver saw her, he would naturally wonder how she knew where to find him. Olivia had wondered the same thing when she had received his text message on the front porch of Antonio's house, *how did he find me?*… for all of *two* seconds. She hadn't questioned that he knew where to find her because that was how their love worked.

"Morning, ma'am," a young man with a scruffy face and bruised eyes said, approaching her as she stepped toward the waiting El train.

"I don't have any change," she said.

He smiled with half of his teeth missing and his gums drooping – *meth?* – and offered a simple "Thank you, have a nice day," before walking toward his next prospect.

The train's cabin was chilly; the doors remained open to accept additional passengers and allowed the cool spring air inside. Olivia sat in a seat closer to the end of the cabin. Without much reception on her phone, she scrolled through her pictures. In the first one, she saw Carlo smiling with a beer in his hand at a tent party. The next pic was Carlo on the beach, bent over to help a young child with his sand castle, half of his ass hanging out of his swimming trunks. Olivia laughed at that pic. The next one she had taken during an open-roof cruise in his Benz SLK; the desert mountains in the background, and a scowl on his face, which was shaded by the bill of his favorite baseball cap. She remembered that drive, remembered the argument when he suggested marriage and starting a family. She also remembered how he had veered off the road and fucked her after that argument, leaning her over the trunk and taking her doggy style at an abandoned service station on the side of the highway.

The CTA chime *dinged* and the doors closed, but Olivia took one last look at the man whose heart she had broken that day in the desert before tucking her phone away. It still stung to think that she had left him like she had, but here she was.

In Chicago.

She had come for Oliver and that wasn't fair to Carlo. It was unfair that for all of these years she had split her heart into two – one piece for Carlo which allowed her to enjoy life and forget about the past, and another piece that belonged solely to *herself*, and that was the same piece that allowed her to *feel* because it was the same piece that belonged to Oliver.

Staring out the train window at the nearly abandoned Kennedy Expressway, Olivia admitted to herself that she was here specifically because at this moment in her life, no matter what casualties she might leave in her wake, she was here to *feel* again. She was committed to spending the rest of her life feeling and loving. No more burying that stuff deep, deep down.

Realizing that her eyes had teared up, she grabbed her phone and checked her messages. A quiet note from Carlo waited for her, but she refused to read it. She tucked the phone away and continued staring out the window, even when they entered the subway tunnels. She didn't look away until the train reached Washington, where she disembarked and rose to street level outside the Richard J. Daley Center. She looked around, getting her bearings before heading toward North Michigan Ave where her hotel was. No more Drake Hotel for her.

} i {

Once Olivia settled into her room, she indulged in a quick nap, showered, then ordered a cab to take her to Winnetka, where Oliver lived. She knew he was still making trips to Barney's, a small coffee shop that reminded her of that old television show, Cheers, because the ladies there loved him and called him by his name. And she also knew that he made his weekend visits for a cappuccino in the mid-afternoon while his wife was out with her racquet club friends and the kids were doing some activity or other.

"You from around here?" the cab driver asked.

"I am now," she said. And she meant it. She had every intention of staying in Chicago until Oliver agreed to spend the rest of his life with her.

"Welcome to Chicago, you'll love it here."

"Thanks," she said, but the reality was that she would love it anywhere so long as Oliver were there too.

The taxi stopped outside of Barney's. After paying him and tossing in a ten-dollar tip because he was excited, Olivia checked the time. She had plenty of time. So once inside, she ordered a large latté and a dessert. She settled at the table in the back corner so she could see everyone coming into the building but not be in the cross-hairs of anyone's attention, then retrieved her MacBook so she could start writing.

Again.

She hadn't written in years out of spite. Writing meant conferences and conferences meant Oliver and she had wanted to avoid him.

After half an hour of procrastinating on the internet and having written two words ("Chapter One"), she heard the voice that stopped time and life.

"Hey, Trina. Just the medium non-fat cap today," Oliver said with his back to her. The barista said something that made him laugh, but she could tell he had forced that sound. Even after all of these years without hearing his voice or touching him, she could still recognize when he was full of shit.

Olivia considered getting up and approaching him from behind, but then wondered if he might feel her presence here at the coffee shop like she had sensed his that time when he parked across the street from her house. So she stayed silent and watched him from the table. He moved from the cash register to the end of the counter where the espresso machine was. If he looked up, he would see her.

Staring at him from the corner table – she ached at the realization of how long it had been since her lips had touched that face of his – she wondered how long it would take him to notice her. There was more conversation between Oliver and the barista, and then he placed a cap on the disposable cup and started leave.

Her heart rate increased and some flavor of disbelief-inspired tunnel vision clouded her world as she watched him walk to the door without having seen her. She felt the rush of heat plow into her cheeks and had to remind herself to breathe. It had only been a couple of years, yet he was leaving like nothing had ever existed between them. Like they hadn't been in this exact same coffee shop before, just the two of them and their love. The history alone should have caused him to look at this corner table, yet he hadn't even glanced.

Had she been wrong about him? About their love?

But-

With his hand on the door, Oliver stopped.

Olivia wondered why he had paused, why he continued to stand there with his back to her and why he hadn't turned around and taken a running spider-monkey leap at her (not that a man would do that kind of thing, it was more appropriate for a woman, but still).

"Oliver," she said under her breath, surprised by how much the word hurt.

Finally, she watched his shoulders rise and fall as he inhaled a deep breath, then he just shook his head like he didn't know what he was thinking, and stepped outside, the bell above the door chiming as he left.

And Olivia sat there, unable to breathe or think or see straight, like someone had just punched a hole in her chest and ripped her heart out.

Chapter 17

The barista stepped out from behind the counter and approached Olivia, the bell above the door settling into silence now that Oliver had left. The younger woman carried a small piece of paper, and when Olivia noticed her approaching, the woman's face turned sober-as-fuck, real fast. But she didn't slow down, didn't turn around and run the other way, which was what Olivia had been hoping for.

"You're Olivia," the woman said. She placed the piece of paper on the table, face-up so Olivia could see that it was a picture.

Of her.

"He's been waiting." With a sideways nod toward the door where Oliver had just left, the barista added: "You need to go after him."

"I… can't," Olivia choked out.

The barista shrugged. "Then you should know he'll be back tomorrow morn-"

Olivia didn't hear the rest of it; she bolted from Barney's, abandoning what remained of her life on the table, and sprinted outside, straight into-

Oliver's arms.

She hadn't seen him standing right outside the door, hadn't noticed that he had placed his cappuccino on the bistro table so that he could pull her tightly into his arms once she sprinted outside. He had ambushed her, and as much as this frustrated her, it also alarmed her.

"I have you," he whispered into her ear, then brushed her hair out of his way so he could kiss her neck. "I have you. Again."

She squeezed him so tightly that she feared she might suffocate him, but she didn't care. If he died in her arms, she would die right there along with him because this embrace confirmed for her that her sole purpose for being here – not "here" as in Chicago, but "here" as in this life – was Oliver.

"Don't let me go," she begged, her voice hitching as his lips pressed against that spot on her neck that made her wet, every time. The jerk had remembered everything, hadn't he?

"I live with every little detail of you," he confessed, as if he had just read her mind. "Only you're more perfect now than you've ever been."

She told him she couldn't live without him, and he agreed that he couldn't live without her either. To Olivia, it felt like a scene straight out of high school, except they were both older. Much older.

When Oliver finally let her down and out of his arms, he asked what she was doing in Chicago.

"I've come for you," she said. And then she laughed. Not a crazy-lover kind of laugh, just a regular laugh because she hadn't explained herself properly. "Not like that," she assured him. "We've got a few years left in that promise of ours. I just want to be close. Close enough that the moment you're single, you're all mine. I can't waste another minute without you, and if it means sitting on the sidelines until I'm called into the game, whether it's now or in the ninth inning, I'm willing to wait."

The way Oliver's face twisted and tightened suggested that he didn't seem to like what she had just said. So Olivia shrugged and told him about her writing. "I need to get back to it. So I sold my shares in the mortgage brokerage and I'm using the money to launch my writing career again. I have a few years of salary saved up, Oliver. I'll be okay. And I'm not here to pressure you. But maybe the occasional lunch, or Bulls game, or night out at the movies… maybe that will be enough to keep me happy. And enough to remind you that I'm here and I'm never going away again."

He opened his arms, and she melted against his chest again, breathing him in with long, deep gulps of air. She felt whole for the first time in years, right here in his embrace.

"I'm not here to interrupt anything."

He held her at an arm's length and stared into her eyes. "I know. And I'm the happiest I've been in the past…" he rolled his eyes. "Since I last held you."

There was rumbling of distant thunder in the background, a complete contradiction to how nicely the otherwise perfect spring afternoon had turned out. The growling interrupted their moment and Olivia felt her stomach tighten at the possibility that her time with Oliver this afternoon had come to an end.

"Now what?" she asked, biting her upper lip. Hard, because she needed reality, and she needed it fast.

He nodded upwardly. "Where are you staying?"

"I have a furnished one-bedroom at West Wacker and North Michigan." She gave him a slick wink, then waved her iPhone at him. "You should come visit me. But text me first." She poked his chest. "I'm going to guess you still have my number after the last message I received... back in Vegas?"

Oliver chuckled nervously as the thunder rolled again behind the approaching clouds. "Listen, about Vegas..." he laughed. "Wait, why aren't you with Antonio? What happened?"

Chapter 18

Walking from the Lake subway stop to Olivia's short-term rental, Oliver questioned the timing of her arrival in Chicago. It was dark and he felt lonely, but he blamed that on their short visit earlier this afternoon before it started raining. He didn't have any other plans tonight; his wife had left for the week, and the kids didn't want to spend much time with him anymore these days.

      Once in the lobby, he texted Olivia a simple message – *I'm here* – and then sat in one of the lobby chairs. He waited for a few minutes, nervous about the purpose of this visit. After Toronto, as Olivia started to take her relationship with Antonio a lot more seriously, Oliver had given up on these sexual encounters. He wondered why Olivia complained about splitting her heart between two men and so easily dismissed his own difficulties with it. Although he and his wife had a healthy sex life, it gutted him to want and imagine Olivia while his wife straddled him and did the things she did. He hated that each time he slept with his wife, he felt like he was cheating on Olivia. It was backwards and it occurred to him that the reason it bothered Olivia so much was that, in her world, she was cheating on Antonio.

When he looked up from his lap, he saw her standing there. The sight of her impressed him. Not because of her absolute beauty – she had aged – but because he felt the closeness of her. In her jeans and casual sweater, she looked about as normal as anyone else... but she was *there*.

"Wow," he breathed, standing up and giving her a brief hug.

"I'm not hungry," she said, which he found to be an interesting response to his *wow* statement.

So they went upstairs. They watched television. They ate snacks. They talked about everything, picking up where they had left off the last time they were together. It was as though mere minutes separated this moment from the last one they had, not years.

"This whole time," he said at last, "I wondered whether you ever loved me at all."

"Why? How could you question that?"

"You disappeared. You wanted nothing to do with me."

Olivia sat directly beside him, her hip pressed up against his as she took his shoulder and forced him to look at her. "I fought to hate you. I fought to forget about you. And I think I did a good job of burying you in my past and convincing myself that you belonged there. But do you know where I was wrong? Where the biggest lie was?"

"It killed me to think of you having happiness with another man," he said. He had struggled with that, but ultimately knew she could never love Antonio the way she loved, or claimed to love, him.

"The biggest lie I told myself was that you would never be my present or future, Oliver." She closed her eyes and kissed his lips, her tongue sliding across his before retracting. "The biggest lie was that time separated us. It's not time. It's not. It's *us*. We are what separate us. And I'm done being the problem, Oliver. I'm here until you're ready. I'm here for either the scraps of you or for all of you, and everything in between."

He felt a jolt of something he could only describe as *electrical* course through his body, and had to stand and walk away. "I need the bathroom."

Olivia seemed to have felt it too; she stood and pointed him toward the front door. "On the left." And then she paced – Oliver watched her in the mirror on the backside of the main door.

Steering into the bathroom, he hit the lights and stared at himself in the mirror. His reflection scared him – pale face, sunken eyes, smile lines around his mouth, the thickening sprinkles of gray at his temples. He found nothing attractive about himself and knew that *time* might not have separated them, but it was certainly running out. Their love might extend across their past, present and future, but there was only so much time left for them to enjoy it.

Twisting the faucet, he splashed a bit of water on his face, his nerves burning like acid in his gut.

"What am I doing here?" he asked.

After drying his face with a hand towel, he returned to the main living area, unbuttoning his shirt to reveal the graying on his chest. The decision to leave his wife had happened somewhere between the faucet and the moment Olivia leapt into his arms, wrapping her legs around his waist and slamming her face against his. He stumbled toward the only other room in the small apartment, kicking the door open and dropping her onto the mattress.

"I love you, Oliver," she said, raising her hips and

working herself out of her jeans.

Oliver tore the pants away and went straight to her panties. He pressed his thumb against her clit, massaged it in a circular motion as he kissed a path along the inside of her thighs, nibbling down at each stop before moving closer to her pussy. But once he was close enough, he didn't let her fuck his mouth. Instead, he slid her panties aside and let her glide herself onto his thumb while he climbed higher on top of her.

"Take your sweater off."

When she stopped moving her hips against his hand, he withdrew his thumb and sucked her juices away.

"Fuck me, Oliver," she begged, tearing her sweater and bra away.

He pushed her onto her back and began fondling her breasts, then kissing her nipples before moving his hand back to the wet mess between her legs, and as he slid his fingers inside her, she moaned.

"Oh, fuck, Oliver!"

Her body quivered beneath him and he felt her muscles contract around his fingers.

Oliver had never known a hard-on like this before. He removed his fingers and stroked the length of his dick, groaning at the sensation of her juices along his shaft.

"I want you inside me," Olivia begged, raising her hips off of the mattress and rubbing herself against him, hoping to entice him. "Please."

He pushed her back down onto the mattress, then lay against her, careful to not enter her just yet. Sliding his hand up the length of her spine, he grabbed a handful of hair and tugged gently.

"Oliver," she panted. "I want to come with you."

"I love you," he whispered, then reached down with his free hand and teased her with the tip of his dick.

"More," she pleaded. "I love you more."

She rolled her hips and jerked her body in such a way that he slid easily inside, her warmth enveloping him instantly. After her first hungry thrust, she moaned. Fuck, he missed the sounds and smells and tastes of Olivia. He pulled on her hair again, elevating the volume of her moans as he pounded into her. And by yanking on her hair, he forced her to arc her neck, revealing that special spot where he could cause an instant orgasm.

But he spared her.

Instead, he pressed his lips and tongue to the pulsating vein, the one that rose from her collarbone and created a path directly to her jaw. He licked that line and once his lips found hers, and he felt her muscles tightening around him in short, sudden bursts.

Then he lost it.

No, not *it*, but himself. He lost all of himself to Olivia.

And this time, it was forever.

Chapter 19

Mike was a good guy, tall with a beautiful tan and a bank account that might not be able to buy happiness, but it could certainly buy a lot of smiles and memories. Olivia liked him and felt that she could probably even love him someday. The way things had ended with Oliver a few months ago when he didn't show up at Barney's like he was supposed to, she once again questioned whether he would follow through. And yes, he had been right: they were getting older. Mike could make this last half (or less) of her life enjoyable and happy. Well, happy enough.

She couldn't wait for Oliver.

She couldn't die alone.

So she tried things out with Mike. Tonight, they had spent some time at the Navy Pier, at a private jazz club, and then at a martini bar. It was three o'clock in the morning when Mike pulled up outside her building in his Porsche. She kissed him hard and he kissed her right back. The look they shared hinted at what could have led to their first night together, but at last, Mike sighed.

"What?" she asked. "Is it me?"

He had an infectious laugh. Shaking his head, he said no. "I just want to do things right with us. You're pretty. Smart. And fucking perfect to my eyes." He shook his head again. "I'm more than a fuck buddy, and I want you to be more than that for me." He patted her leg. "I've got floor tickets for the Bulls tomorrow. Want to help me use them?"

"Thank you, Mike," she said. "You're a gentleman." After kissing him, she promised to join him the following night. When she skipped out of the Porsche, she felt something. It was as if the air had taken on a tinge of... life.

She glanced back at the Porsche and waved. Mike signaled back and drove off.

Inside the elevator, she wondered how often she had thought about Oliver tonight. Even with Mike, who dulled the pain that she felt whenever she filed Oliver back into her past, Olivia knew she couldn't escape him completely. She never would.

And once she opened the door to her small apartment, she knew why.

"Oliver," she breathed, and for the first time in her life, she wished he *hadn't* shown up, standing in the foyer of the small apartment like an apparition. "Why are you here? How'd you get in?"

"It's over," he said, then sobbed into his hands before collapsing to his knees. "It's over."

Suddenly, she felt her own knees weaken. Their entire story flashed across her memory in a moment filled with fear, and she hated herself for the sacrifices she had made: the career, Carlo Antonio, the kids she would never have (Oliver's kids), the white-picket fence, the happiness, everything. Her throat constricted as she stepped forward, dropping to the floor mere inches from the man she had loved from the moment she first met him, the moments together and apart, the promises kept and broken. She loved this man in ways that could never be explained because that kind of love extended beyond humanity and life.

"It's over," he repeated, his body convulsing.

"Oliver," she said, but her words came out in choked whispers. "What's gone on?"

She wrapped her arms around him to calm him, then brushed her hand along his back.

"What happened?"

He didn't speak for a long time, and this scared

Olivia. She wondered if the air had changed because her life was about to change.

"Oliver…"

When his body calmed in her arms, she asked him again what was going on, what had happened.

"I left her." He gulped. "I broke her heart to save…"

"Oliver…"

"I broke my wife's heart to save my own." He sobbed a little more, and when he finished, he held her face so he could stare deep into her eyes. "I can't risk losing you again, Olivia. If you'll take me back, I'm yours until the end of time." He paused to catch his breath. "I'm yours anyway, but I won't truly live if I breathe one more wasted moment without you."

She considered his words. Despite the sincerity in his eyes, she had a good thing going with Mike. It was new, yes. But it wasn't broken, it wasn't *this*.

"Don't bury me," he begged. "Don't bury *us* in the past, Olivia."

Oliver was right. This could be their only time together. Right now.

"What?" he asked. "You're quiet. You haven't said

much."

There was a beat before she pulled his face to hers, kissing him and sending the only message he needed to hear: he was home.

Epilogue

Hope stopped at the traffic light and checked her phone. No messages, no texts. So she scrolled through her photos, sliding her finger across each image until she arrived at one pic in particular. A young man with glasses and a face that needed a razor smiled back at her, his teeth shining. She remembered running her tongue across those teeth in search of his. The memory made her happy.

A *promise*?

When the driver in the BMW behind her leaned on his horn, she snapped her attention upward, and then made a dangerous U-turn. More horns, but she kicked down on the gas to get farther away, faster.

She had a promise on her mind and she needed to honor it.

Fuck, what was she doing? Thinking?

As she drove above the speed limit toward Morgan Barker's employer, she called home. She knew Matt wouldn't answer, knew he wasn't even home and would not make it there for a few more days. And after that, it would be a few more before he flew to Chicago for his big two-week assignment.

When the answering system picked up, she left a brief message.

"Hey, Matt. I, uh, I got called out to another audit risk, so I'll have to catch up with you in Chicago. Might only be for a few days, but once I know my schedule a little better, I'll let you know." She gave a sigh, a guilty one because she hated lying to her fiancé. He wouldn't know any different, though – guilt for the lie, or guilt for having to cancel at the last minute, it was all the same. "Safe travels, Matt. I... I love you."

She disconnected and pressed the End button several times over, just to be safe.

A couple of blocks later, she steered into the business district and stopped her rental outside the front doors to the building where Morgan worked. She let the engine run, sitting still behind the wheel and thinking through the problems swirling around in her head. She knew Emma's story. She knew Oliver and Olivia's story. And now she had some questions about her own story that only Morgan could answer.

Reaching into the roller briefcase in the back seat,

she came out with a binder and located Morgan Barker's business card. He had written his cell phone number on the front of it a couple of weeks ago. He answered with an abrupt: "Barker."

"Did you read it?"

Silence.

"How about we get an early start on lunch?" Hope suggested, quoting his words. "I'm parked outside."

At last, she heard a sigh on his end of the line. She had expected that. "Five minutes, Hope. I'll be there in five minutes."

While waiting for Morgan, Hope made one more call. To her travel agent. "Hey, it's me again. I'm sorry, but I need to reinstate those original travel plans." She listened to the clacking and then acknowledged the $200 fee it would cost to make the flight and hotel changes. Again. "Actually, I was hoping to book something a little different. Just a different hotel. I was thinking of the Fairmont. Can you arrange that?"

As the travel agent confirmed the reservation changes, she heard the knocking on the passenger side and glanced over to find Morgan staring at her through the window. She poked the power locks and thanked the travel agent as Morgan settled into the passenger seat. He seemed a little nervous and the shadow along his jawline suggested that he had a little more than the recent IRS issues on his mind.

"What the fuck is this?" he asked.

Hope knocked the transmission into Drive and pulled away. "Did you ever eat that sandwich, Morgan?"

He turned his hands over in his lap, staring into his palms before chuckling and shaking his head. "Fuck no. I wasn't hungry."

"So you read the novel." She drove the rental in silence, her decision already made but she wanted to hear it from Morgan. "What did you think about the new ending?"

"It's not new. They always ended up together. You just didn't write the full fucking ending, Hope."

She stayed quiet until they reached the gourmet sandwich place. Killing the engine, she reached across the armrest and placed a hand on Morgan's forearm as he made to get out of the car. The gesture stopped him and when he looked back at her, his eyes revealed brokenness. The sight shocked her, as if she had just stared into the eyes of a ghost. She turned her attention away as Morgan settled back into the passenger seat.

"What's up, Hope? You wanna fuck me?" He flashed a smile; the emotion he attempted to portray with his mouth contradicted the emotion on the rest of his face.

"Forget it." She sighed. "Let's eat."

"No, hold the fuck up," he said, laughing. "What's going on here?"

She gave it some thought. At last, her stomach growled and she knew that outside of whatever snacks they served aboard the flight to Chicago, she would not have a chance to eat again until tomorrow. "Morgan, let's eat."

They moved from the car and into the restaurant, which was relatively empty given the time of day so they had their choice of booth.

"Same one as last time?" Hope asked, waving toward the booth. "Is that okay?"

"Sure. Whatever."

Hope sat first, clasping her hands on the table and watching Morgan move with the dexterity and swiftness of a geriatric tortoise. He looked old, really old. Maybe that sudden aging explained the silence that settled between them.

"Morgan, how does this really end?"

"You know how it ends. After Oliver proposes,

Olivia gets real fucking sick and..."

"No, not *Our Story*."

He shrugged, like he suddenly found himself at a complete loss for words.

The waitress came for their orders and they snapped a quick response so they could get back to whatever this conversation meant. But Hope didn't jump back in just yet. She watched him, the way he blinked with increased frequency and stared out the corners of those gray eyes.

Hope had her answer. She checked the time. Three hours until her departure, and she felt anxious now.

Morgan raised his hands to his face and sobbed, and all Hope could do was watch him. And wait for the broken words to fall out of his mouth.

"I miss her. I fucking miss my Emma. Why won't she text me? Or find me?" He ugly-cried for a little longer, each racking sob reinforcing her decision about this upcoming trip. "I want her arms around me. Her lips on mine. I wish I could smell her and taste her and just fucking be with her again." He stared straight at her for a beat. "I want Emma."

When he calmed down, he used a napkin to wipe at

his face, then forced an embarrassed chuckle.

Shrugging, he said, "I don't know how it ends. But I know I miss her and every fiber in my body aches for her."

They shared another silent moment, but the excitement for her upcoming trip bubbled up inside her and rolled out in the form of laughter.

Morgan smiled. "How about you, Hope? How does it end for you?"

She laughed a little more, apologized and somehow swallowed that giddiness deep down. "I'm sorry," she said again. Then, refocusing her energy and dropping into her serious mode, she told him. "My ending starts tomorrow. And it's a happy one, Morgan. I might have given you that story, but I'm not you, I'm nothing like you. I'm not going to sit here and wonder what my 'Emma' is doing and why mine won't come running after me like I'm a vulnerable lamb that needs saving." She pressed a hand to her chest. "I'm going to chase my 'Emma' because we belong together and there's no other ending to my story."

"Are you a fucking lesbian?"

"You're an asshole," Hope pointed out, grabbing her purse because she couldn't sit here and eat with him. She had come for an answer and no matter how hungry she would be tonight once she arrived in Chicago, she wasn't here to stuff food into her face. "His name is Cameron. And if I know anything, it's that love is the easy part. But relationships? Those take work."

"Where are you going?"

"Home. I'm going home." She started walking away, but glanced back. "And you need to go home, too. To Emma."

THE END

Non Friction – Preview

If you liked *Hope*, check out *Non Friction*. While *Hope* explores the "middle" section of Olivia and Oliver's love story, *Non Friction* provides the beginning and end of their story, as well as how *Our Story* was first conceived (as Morgan Barker's initiative to earn back his wife's love).

Here is a short excerpt from *Non Friction*. Buy it in paperback or ebook format at Amazon.com.

PROLOGUE

Our Story

As a child, Oliver Weaver often confused the John Hancock Center with the Sears Tower. It happened mostly with tourists or people unfamiliar with Chicago. Both structures were tall, dark and beautiful, and they were both essential landmarks in one of the country's most impressive cities – Batman Rises and Dark Knight were filmed there, for instance. But that night so many years long after his childhood had faded into a single memory of "everything before Olivia," sitting at a window table of the Signature Room on the ninety-fifth floor of the John Hancock, Oliver Weaver recognized that drawing similarities between two distinct objects of beauty was something he had always done.

While the waitress took Olivia's order, Oliver watched the way his date's lips moved somewhat crookedly when she spoke, the way her long and slender fingers brushed her hair behind her ear to give him an uninterrupted appreciation of her face. He memorized every feature like his life depended on it. And although this woman was not his wife, making a comparison between them was finally something he refused to do.

"The views are amazing up here," Olivia Warren told him once the waitress left. She wore bright red lipstick and a semi-formal dress that he preferred to imagine on the floor of her hotel room rather than draped over her petite figure. "Have you always lived here?"

He admitted to spending his entire life in Chicago – elementary school five miles West from here, a semi-private, faith-based high school in Wilmette, and finally college at Northwestern, followed by his MBA at Kellogg right before his youngest was born. "And you? Has Vegas always been home?"

Their conversation went on in this manner for most of their meal. Innocent and ultimately meaningless, but it meant something- no, it meant everything to Oliver because he knew their time together would end sooner than it should.

When they finished their dessert, they strolled N. Michigan Ave under the lights – walking past Macy's and Burberry as they headed South on the one side of the street, and past the Grand Lux Café, Hershey and the Water Tower as they headed North on the other.

"It's not Vegas," he admitted, holding her hand as they walked, "but it's alive. I always love this part of town after a nice dinner."

Olivia sighed. "I had a wonderful time with you, Oliver."

At the lobby of her hotel, they stopped and stared. They were still holding hands, still smiling from that first moment they truly saw each other. He noticed a glimmer in her eyes that reminded him of the stars or, more appropriately, the lights on N. Michigan Ave a few minutes ago and a single word came to mind: alive. He knew he had the same glow in his own eyes because Olivia made him feel that way: alive.

"I hope to see you again, Oliver," she said.

"You will. I promise." Not soon enough.

They hugged, holding on a little tighter and longer than newly acquainted people normally would, but then again they were more than just two people. When they finally pulled themselves apart, Oliver could tell she didn't want to let go of their time together. He didn't want to let go either.

"Come up to my room?" she suggested.

At that moment, Oliver knew that his decision would do more than just haunt him for the rest of his life – it would forever change it. More than that, it would change him, his personality, his character, everything he ever believed in and loved and cherished.

So when he agreed to accompany this beautiful woman to her hotel room, he knew that some decisions in life are made before you ever have a chance to think them through. And sometimes that's a good thing.

CHAPTER ONE

I always wanted to do something with my life, so when Jennifer decided that our marriage of 12 years, 4 months and 1 ½ weeks just didn't "do it" for her anymore, I figured now was as good a time as any to take that first step. The problem was that if I lacked motivation and direction before her leaving (and I surely did), I didn't even know what those words meant after she left.

As much as I hated her sometimes, I couldn't imagine a moment without her. But I didn't fight her, didn't stop her from packing her shit and all of our daughter's things into our only vehicle – a minivan that embarrassed me, so I was fine with her taking it just like she had taken the last twelve years of my life –

and drove off to some secret place she refused to tell me about. I figured if she wanted to learn the hard way that leaving me was making the biggest mistake of her life, so be it. I could give her a bit of space, no problem.

"Princess, where are you going?" I had asked a dozen times or so on that day, probably way more, but I stopped counting.

"None of your fucking business."

The way Jennifer kept her lips sealed, you'd think she worked for the CIA instead of the local hospital.

I expected her home within a day. After a week, I started to worry. Two weeks, I became a mess. Reality sunk in hard and fast.

And those nights of sunk-in reality sucked. A lot.

I couldn't sleep for more than a few hours at a time; I had chest pains and thought I was going to die; I lost track of what day and month it was. I ached for Princess's body in our bed. And I actually missed Evelyn yelling for someone to cover her up because her blankets had rolled off of her four-year old body in the middle of some dream about whatever it was that kids her age dream about - marshmallows, Barbies, whatever.

Alone in the house, I took the blankets Jennifer had left behind, rolled them up into a body pillow and slept with them.

I called in sick at work. A lot. Sometimes I forgot to make the actual call, which my boss didn't appreciate too much.

And in those lonely moments of self-pity, I began to realize that I really needed to dig deep. I had to find motivation and direction, start doing something with my life because that would get me back on track.

And maybe once that happened and Jennifer saw how much better I was, she might even return. Yes, she might move her stuff back, start bitching at me again about all the crap that went wrong in her day. That was what I wanted, more than anything.

So I finally summoned the motivation I needed (to win Jennifer back, to get her and our daughter back into our home) but I didn't know what to do with it. Where do people go with their motivation?

I needed to get laid; that seemed to be the logical place where most newly divorced men my age started. I figured I was no different.

Acknowledgments

A novel's failure is the fault of many people, not just the author's. So this is where I point fingers at the people who have made it a failure. Incidentally, if this novel turns into a success, they can share in the success as well.

Amy Louise Clark – you're my loudest cheerleader and no matter how many times I step up to that ledge and try to jump, you hold me back and keep me going. Thank you for believing in my stories and for sharing my vision.

Jennifer Clark Sell – your ability to accommodate me on such short notice means more to me than you'll ever know. Thank you for your expertise, time and effort and, well, everything.

Kelsey Burns – you read my stories and call me out. On everything. That makes me stronger as a writer. So if there is ever an Indie Writer's UFC tournament, you better bet on me.

The Top-Secret Morganettes Group. You ladies are so incredibly supportive. This story was inspired by you and was written for you. Your feedback and ongoing support has humbled me and reminds me why I write in the first place. No novella or acknowledgments paragraph could ever adequately thank you.

To all of the bloggers and readers who write about my stories. There's a reason the publishing industry is undergoing such a transformational change, and you're the reason authors are forced to rethink their roles in the storytelling process. Thanks to your efforts, this industry has evolved from a one-way conversation to an engaging one that relies heavily on collaboration and feedback. You've caused this improvement and continue to challenge the way stories are told, shared, and enjoyed.

Printed in Great Britain
by Amazon.co.uk, Ltd.,
Marston Gate.